THE KNIGHTS
OF THE
ROUND TABLE

Translated by Lee Ann Bortolussi

Award Publications Limited

Many are the kings of the past whose stories are retold today. Few, however, can boast of the immense popularity that one king has always enjoyed, and will continue to enjoy for quite some time to come - the famous King Arthur of the fantastic realm of legendary England, Logris.

Called to the service of the royal power directly by God, through the famous stratagem of the sword in the stone, this young king, just sixteen years old at the time, finds himself involved in a series of interminable adventures. He travels his kingdom far and wide in all directions, protecting good and fighting evil. Later on, he basks in his glory, and earns fame and great wisdom as well.

These tales contain many other characters, some magical, some not, but all are cloaked in immortal fame like their king. There is the beautiful and sweet Queen Guinevere, the prodigal Launcelot, and the faithful and unfortunate Merlin the Magician, a very wise man who becomes incapable when faced with the perils of love. In addition to these wonderful characters, there is also the envious and cruel Queen Morgana le Fay, King Arthur's sister. She is the one who causes the fratricidal war that will bring about the end of the glorious era of the Knights of the Round Table. As we will soon see, it was certainly a time of magic and enchantment.

When King Arthur dies, a hand mysteriously appears from the lake and takes the magical sword found in the stone, Excalibur, back to the enchanted land that it came from. Maybe this is where the knights have also gone, and where they continue to live today, proud and fearless, unfortunately departed from our world forever.

Many are the versions passed down through the ages of this ancient "Arthurian Cycle" of legends, which probably dates to the twelfth century. Its actual origins, however, are buried deep in the meandering historical web of English and French Literature. Here follows the romantic story of the fascinating adventures of the knights and their lovely damsels.

THE SWORD IN THE STONE

On Saint Martin's Day, many centuries ago, the great king, Uther-Pendragon died in his castle of Camelot, in the capital of the kingdom of Logris. He left neither widow nor children, and thus his crown was without an heir.

The barons and the bishops of Great Britain, who had come to the castle for the funeral, were very worried. The people of Logris were also very pre-occupied. A kingdom without a king is like a ship without a navigator. Who would be their new king?

Quite a few of the barons would have deserved to be king. None of them dared to step forward, however, to ask openly for the crown. So they decided to ask advice of Merlin, a great and wise magician, who knew all about the past and who could see into the future as well. Merlin advised them to wait until Christmas Day, and, in the meantime, to pray to God for wisdom.

When Christmas Day arrived, all of the barons and all of the people of Camelot joined together in the cathedral to celebrate mass. As soon as the Archbishop had given the benediction, everyone came out of the church. All marveled to find a large stone and an anvil from which a sword was protruding, sitting in the middle of the square. No one was able to explain such a mystery. The Archbishop, who was very upset by this occurrence, went quickly to the stone and there he found these words inscribed:

"Whoever shall remove this sword from the anvil is right wise king - born of England."
Immediately the strongest among the barons stepped forward and requested to remove the sword. One by one they gripped the sword and tried to remove it, but in vain.

THE KING OF LOGRIS

In the meantime, the great New Year's Day tournament was about to begin. In a large field near the town, the arena had been set up, and all around this the most important barons had set up their tents. Many others had found lodging in the inns of Camelot. Among the barons, Sir Ector had also come with his two sons, Kay and Arthur.
The first and elder son, Kay was twenty years old and had just recently been knighted. The younger son was just sixteen years old, and acted as his brother's page. As Kay left to go to the tournament, he realized that he had forgotten his sword. So he said to Arthur, "Please return to the inn and bring me my sword." But the town was deserted, and everyone was out to watch the tournament. All of the shops were closed, including the inn. Arthur could not get in. "What shall I do?" he said to himself. Looking about, he noticed the sword in the stone. Knowing nothing of the sword and its history, he approached the sword, took it in his hands, and pulled . . . and the sword came out of the anvil as if it had been pulled from its sheath!
Satisfied with what he had done, Arthur galloped his steed toward the tournament field and presented the sword to his brother. "This is a very beautiful sword Arthur, but it is not mine," said Kay. "Where did you find it?" "It was stuck in an anvil, in the main square. . ." Kay, amazed, went straight to Ector to tell him what had happened, and Ector, also stupefied, turned to Arthur. "Is it true, my son, that you extracted this sword from the anvil?" he asked. "Yes, my father, that is the truth. Why? Have I committed a sin?" "Hurry, return straight to

6

Camelot," said Ector, "put the sword back where you found it, and promise me that you will not tell a single soul what has happened."

That evening, when the tournament was over, all of the barons went to church for the prayer of vespers. Ector asked the Archbishop if Arthur could be permitted to try to remove the sword from the stone. "This boy? But he is not even a knight!" exclaimed the Archbishop. "Let him try, I beg you," responded Ector. "All right, but he will be the laughing stock of the town," replied the Archbishop. And as predicted,

when Arthur approached the stone, laughter was heard throughout the square. But silence fell when everyone saw that Arthur could remove the sword without any effort!

All of the people bowed down to him, as did many of the barons. Some remained standing, however. "He is just a boy," exclaimed one of the barons. "He is the son of a common knight. How could we possibly accept him as our king?" said another. And then yet another baron added, "Beware! It could have been a trick!" So the Archbishop ordered Arthur to put the sword back into the anvil. "Now we shall all see whether or not this has been a trick. Whoever wishes, let him attempt to remove the sword!" Once again, one by one, the barons tried to extract the sword, but all attempts were in vain.

However, when Arthur tried again the sword slipped right out of the anvil. "On your knees, before the sign of God!" intoned the Archbishop. The barons who did not kneel the first time, however, remained standing. "We cannot accept a king who is not of royal lineage!" they said in unison. The Archbishop immediately replied, "It is God who shall elect our king. Whoever among you accepts His sign shall follow me." All but the eleven rebellious barons followed the Archbishop into the cathedral, where he picked up the crown and solemnly placed it on the head of young Arthur.

EXCALIBUR

"Father, what has happened?" Arthur asked of Ector. Ector responded, "Sire, you have received the crown that is your right." "What? You call me Sire? Are you not my father? And you, Kay, my brother?" inquired Arthur. "We are first of all your devoted servants, sire," they both replied. "What shall I do now?" asked Arthur. "Go to your castle and close the doors, because you have enemies. Then hold high court, sire," suggested Ector. King Arthur followed his father's advice.

To hold high court meant to invite to the castle all of the noble gentlemen of the kingdom. The young king received an oath of faith from the bishops and the barons, except from the eleven who had rebelled, and who protested still. When Merlin the Magician appeared in the hall, there was much confusion. "What is going on, gentlemen? Why all of this yelling?" "We do not want young Arthur as our king!" they answered. "Ah, then you do not believe that he deserves the throne of Logris? You are wrong. He is in fact the son of King Uther-Pendragon." When Merlin said this, everyone fell silent. Then he said, "Uther-Pendragon was in love with the beautiful Duchess Igraine and asked me to help him to marry her, using my magical powers. I agreed, but on one condition: that he would give his first-born child to me. When the queen gave birth to a beautiful baby boy, I arrived at the castle and took the child away." Everyone was amazed by this story. Merlin continued. "After one year, I gave the child, whose name was Arthur, to the good knight, Ector, who had just lost a one year-old son. Is this not true, Ector?" Ector replied,

"It is." "Thus Arthur grew up the son of Ector, but he is actually the son of King Uther-Pendragon, and is of royal blood. Whoever does not swear fidelity to him will be his enemy, and will be fought in battle." Again, all of the barons kneeled before the king, except for the eleven rebels. As they left, there were threats of war and death. When Arthur discovered that he was not Ector's son, he was very upset. There was no time, however, to dwell on this because a messenger arrived. He said to the king, "Sire, the barons who have rebelled are preparing to attack the castle." "What will we do?" asked Arthur. Merlin the Magician said, "Take the sword that came from the anvil; its name is Excalibur, which means 'To Sever Iron and Steel'. Then gather your men and go to battle."

KING ARTHUR'S VICTORY

The faithful barons gathered quickly. The young king wore his armor, but refused to wear a helmet so that all could see his face and his blond locks. He mounted his great steed, raised Excalibur and shouted, "Follow me, I am going to battle!" The faithful knights obeyed, and King Arthur showed himself to be so valorous that all were amazed. The rebels were defeated and many were killed. Any of them who happened to survive swore on bended knee to be faithful to King Arthur, the true king.

THE BATTLE AGAINST THE KING OF THE DESOLATE LANDS

Within a year King Arthur was recognized as the legitimate King of Logris by all of the other kings and gentlemen of Great Britain. He lived in the castle with Ector and Kay, his step-brother, who was elected seneschal, or grand counselor. Merlin the Magician gave him advice and instruction. From Merlin, Arthur learned to rule with prudence and wisdom and thus the people of Logris became very devoted to their king. The barons of the realm, who knew of his valor, began to appreciate his many good qualities.

The fame of the young king exceeded the boundaries of Great Britain and even Brittany, across the ocean. Two good brothers, Ban and Bors, rulers of Benwick and Ganis respectively, came to pay homage to King Arthur.

All of a sudden a breathless messenger arrived in the throne room. "Sire," he said, "in the name of the sacred sword Excalibur, go and assist my master King Leodegrance of Cameliard! He has been threatened by Claudas, King of the Desolate Lands, and he sends word to you that he will truly lose his kingdom unless you help him!" "The King of the Desolate Lands is our enemy!" exclaimed Ban and Bors. "So he will be my enemy as well," said King Arthur. A few days later, the three kings and their knights presented themselves to King Leodegrance in the realm of Cameliard. They had arrived just in time. Claudas, the King of the Desolate Lands, was advancing at the head of a very strong army. Seeing their numerous and well-aligned enemies approach, Arthur said to Kay, "My brother, this will be a very difficult battle!" It was a very challenging battle. King Claudas was very courageous, and he had many strong men among his followers. There was Froll, the Duke of Germany, an enormous and frightening man. More than once, Arthur, Ban and Bors were in danger of being overcome, and their knights and soldiers seemed ready to turn in flight. But Arthur held Excalibur high, inciting his armies to fight back and to achieve victory.

It was Arthur's battle with the giant Froll that decided the outcome of the war. They fought one-on-one with their spears poised, and then with their swords. They attacked and wounded one another. At one point it seemed as if both would die without either one winning the battle. But in the end, Arthur landed a strong stroke with Excalibur, and wrenched Froll's sword from his hand; Froll had no choice but to turn and flee. Picking up Froll's sword, which was called Marmiadoise, Arthur called out, "Victory!" Hearing this, King Claudas turned his horse and ran. Many of his men followed him, but others surrendered and simply put down their arms.

THE BEAUTIFUL GUINEVERE

King Leodegrance reserved the best of welcomes for the knights who had saved him. Guinevere, his beautiful daughter, washed King Arthur's face and hands which were covered in blood and dust, and dried his brow which was beaded.with perspiration. She also poured red wine for him to drink. As she was doing all of this, the young king was watching her closely, and thought that he had never seen such a beautiful and genteel young maiden. Her hair was very long and blond, and her clear eyes were as green as the sea. Guinevere, on the other hand, had never met a young man so handsome, and so brave on the battlefield. In short, the two fell in love, and just before leaving for Camelot, King Arthur said to King Leodegrance, "I ask for the hand of your daughter, Guinevere." King Leodegrance responded,"If she will have you, I shall be the happiest of men. Guinevere, have you heard? What will your answer be?" Blushing, she responded, "If I shall marry King Arthur I will be the happiest of all women." And so a date was set for the marriage, and for the first time in his life, King Arthur could feel his heart pounding, for he was very much in love.

MERLIN AND VIVIEN

Arthur was not the only one to fall in love at that time. Regardless of his great wisdom, Merlin the Magician had also fallen dangerously in love. As King Arthur was preparing to leave for Camelot, Merlin was to be found walking happily through the forest of Broceland one fine day. It was the most beautiful forest in the world, and there Merlin spied a lovely young maiden sitting next to a clear spring. Her hair was long and dark, her skin was as white as snow, and her lips as red as cherries. Merlin was an old man at this point; his beard was very long and his shoulders a bit curved. So before speaking to the girl, he thought to transform himself into a young page, which he did using one of his magical spells. Then he approached the young girl, and said, "Who are you, fair maiden?" "I am the daughter of the man who owns this land, and my name is Vivien. And you? Might I know your name?" replied Vivien.
"I am but an errant valet, in search of a master who will teach me a trade."
"And what trade might that be?"
"To lift a castle into the air, or to walk on water without wetting my feet."
Vivien laughed, and exclaimed " What a wonderful trade that would be!

Teach me as well, and I will marry you. If I am to your liking, that is."
"Do you really speak the truth?" asked Merlin. "I do," answered Vivien.
So Merlin found a twig and traced a circle on the ground, and worked one of his magical spells. Out of the forest suddenly there appeared a circle of knights and dames who danced to a fife and drum. In the background there appeared a castle made entirely of crystal. Vivien opened her eyes wide with amazement, and her mouth too. She was stupefied. Merlin, who was very much in love with her, said, "See, Vivien? Now will you marry me?" "Oh yes!" she cried. "You must know, however, that I am not as I seem, that I am not a young page, but a man of some years. Just look!" And Merlin transformed himself from a young man to a very old man right before

Vivien's eyes. But she only shrugged and replied, "Only silly young women are influenced by appearances; I will marry you even if you are neither young nor handsome. But you must tell me, right now, who are you?" "I am Merlin the Magician." "Oh! Now I understand all of these enchantments and spells. If you will teach them to me, and explain how I might become wise, I will be your bride." Merlin then extracted a scroll, and on this he wrote some of his rules. "Begin by learning this," he said, "and you will start to know what I know. Now I must go. I shall soon return to take you with me." "I shall wait for you!" replied the young woman. They exchanged a kiss, and Merlin happily went off. Ah, misery! For all of his knowledge, Merlin did not know that he had met love, but at the same time, misfortune.

SIR GAWAINE

In the meantime, at the castle of King Leodegrance, King Arthur was the only one remaining, because King Ban and King Bors had already returned to their realms. Young Arthur was ready to leave for Camelot. He was bidding the lovely Guinevere goodbye, when suddenly Merlin arrived.

"What news do you bring?" asked the king. "Sire, a messenger did inform me not too long ago that the pagan Saxons have disembarked very near to the city of Clarence, and have occupied it. They have sworn that they will kill all of the people of Clarence." Clarence was a city in the realm of Logris. King Arthur was rather disturbed by this news, and he exclaimed, "We must leave here at once."

"We must," continued Merlin, "because the city cannot resist long. But there are too few of us. Many of our knights were wounded in the battle against King Claudas, and the Saxons are so numerous that they could destroy us. We could ask your barons for help, but by the time they arrive Clarence will have been conquered and many of its people will have been killed."

"It is better to die in battle than to leave Clarence to the Saxons!" exclaimed King Arthur. Thus the army left for Clarence. All were worried, because they knew that there were too few of them. Only King Arthur was hopeful. "How can you keep a smile on your face?" Sir Kay said to King Arthur. "We may not survive this battle!"

"Brother, something in my heart tells me that this will not be the case," replied Arthur assuredly.

The next day, a large group of young men on horseback appeared, well-dressed and armed for battle. They

came forward, and when they saw the crest of King Arthur, they dismounted and kneeled before him. "God bless you, Sire. We have come looking for you, to put ourselves in your service. I am Gawaine, and these are my good brothers, Guerrehes and Gaheriet, and these," he continued, motioning to some

of the others, "are Ivan of the White Hands and Ivan the Fair, sons of the King of Gorres; Dodinas le Savage, the son of the King of Sorgalles; Kay, Prince of Estraux and Cahedin, son of King Bran." One by one he named all of his companions. "You are welcome," replied King Arthur, with joy in his heart and his eyes shining. "Before welcoming me, Sire, know that my father was Lot, one of the barons who rebelled against you, and who died in the battle against you." "Even if he was my enemy, Lot was valorous," replied Arthur. "You are welcome, I repeat. From this moment on you are in my service; and I will soon be able to estimate your valor, because we are headed into battle against the pagan

Saxons." This said, and without any further ado, he knighted all of the young men. Then turning to Sir Kay, he added, "Have you seen? There were too few of us, but God has sent us help." Thus heartened by the arrival of Gawaine and the other knights, King Arthur's followers traveled until they were in sight of the city. It was the following morning, and they stopped at the edge of a large field to rest.

Merlin the Magician, who was riding a large hunting steed, raised himself high in his stirrups to look about, and exclaimed "Gentlemen, the Saxons have seen us, and are ready to attack! There are great numbers of soldiers!" King Arthur pulled Excalibur from its sheath and shouted, "Well, we will not sit here and wait for them!" "In the name of noble King Arthur and of Excalibur!" replied all of the knights as they spurred their mounts and set off to attack the enemy.

The Saxons were much more numerous than the knights of King Arthur, and they surrounded them as the waves surround the rocks in the ocean. Nonetheless, they were defeated and forced to flee, both for the valor of the knights of King Arthur, and for the citizens of Clarence, who came out from behind the walls of the city and attacked the Saxons from behind. Frightened and surrounded on all sides, the pagans fled toward the sea, leaving many of their wounded behind on the battlefield. Many pagans also drowned while furiously trying to swim to their ships. "In the name of God, Sire," exclaimed Merlin the Magician, "these young knights have served you very well, especially Sir Gawaine, the son of Lot!"

"Yes, without them we would not have been victorious. Please come here Sir Gawaine," said good King Arthur. The young man obeyed, and the king embraced him. Sir Gawaine was very moved, and exclaimed, "Ah, Sire, you will never have a follower more faithful than I."

THE MARRIAGE OF ARTHUR AND GUINEVERE

The inhabitants of Clarence opened their arms to welcome King Arthur to their city, and they begged him to stay. King Arthur, however, seeing that the town was no longer in danger, decided to return to Camelot. "You are in quite a hurry, Sire," remarked Merlin the Magician. King Arthur replied, "Yes, I am in a hurry to return to my castle, and to my beautiful bride-to-be Guinevere. Remember, I fought this battle in her name."

Just one month later, Arthur and Guinevere celebrated their marriage. Many kings, barons, knights, minstrels, magicians and acrobats arrived for the wedding. There was a large crowd, and the celebrations lasted for three days and three nights.

MERLIN FALLS IN LOVE

Some time later, Merlin informed Arthur and Guinevere that he would be leaving on a trip. He traveled to the forest of Broceland once again, and met with the beautiful Vivien, whom he loved very much. "Finally you have arrived, my dear sir!" exclaimed the maiden. "Promise me that you will never leave again!" Holding hands, they walked for a long time through the forest, exchanging words of love. They then reached the shores of Lake Diana. "Oh," sighed Vivien, "how I would love to live here!" "If it is a house you desire, then a house you shall have," said Merlin. He began to trace magic symbols in the air, and suddenly a beautiful castle arose from the mist of the lake. Vivien remained speechless. Merlin said, "This will be your house. It is invisible to all, except to us and to our friends. This is where we shall live." "Oh Merlin, I am the happiest of women. I beg of you, please tell me how you work such magical spells." Merlin had sworn never to teach any of his magic to anyone. He was so in love, though, that he began to reveal his secrets to Vivien. Day and night he taught her the art of magic. Alas, fool! He who could see into the future could not understand that the young lady did not love him at all. She only wanted to steal his magic secrets and to become a magician as potent as Merlin, or even more so. One day she said to Merlin, "You have taught me many things. But tell me, how can you trap a man inside a castle so that he may never escape?" When he heard this, Merlin felt a pang in his heart. "Ah, Vivien, somehow I feel that this prison you have in mind is for me."

But Vivien answered, "Why do you think such a thing?" "I will teach you what you want to learn," responded Merlin, "but not now because I must return to the kingdom of Logris. Wait for me here, and when I return you will know all that you desire to know." They parted and Merlin returned to the court of King Arthur.

19

THE ROUND TABLE

King Arthur was very pleased that Merlin had returned. For seven days and seven nights, however, the magician was closed in his tower, consulting his tomes of ancient magic. After seven days he presented himself in the great hall. Here he found King Arthur and Guinevere and their knights.

"Sire," said Merlin, "you must know that the Holy Grail, the goblet in which Jesus' blood was gathered, has been taken to Great Britain, and hidden. It will be found by the bravest of knights, and this knight shall be one of yours."

All were silent with amazement. Then Merlin continued. "It is also written that the knights of King Arthur will join together in this hall around a great round table." Suddenly there was thunder and lightning, and the Round Table appeared before them with one-hundred-and-fifty chairs placed all around. On each of the chairs, the name of one knight had been carved on the back in golden letters. There was a name on every chair, except for one. This was the chair of the knight who would find the Holy Grail.

"Whoever should dare to sit in that chair, without being pure of heart," said Merlin, "will risk divine punishment and death. This is the Seat Perilous. Gentlemen, please take your places!" All of the knights seated themselves, but no one dared to occupy the Seat Perilous. Then each one of the knights drew his sword and declared his loyalty to King Arthur.

THE MAIDEN AND THE DWARF

A few days later, while the king was seated at the Round Table, speaking to his knights, a beautiful young maiden suddenly walked into the room. She was holding in her arms a horrible little creature: a hairy dwarf with a beard and a hunched back, crossed eyes and bow legs. Everyone was amazed and a bit embarrassed, for it seemed that the young maiden was in fact quite fond of the dwarf. Then the maiden spoke. "I salute you, Sire. I am Bianna, daughter of King Calmadieu, and I have come from very far away to ask a favor of you." "Speak," replied King Arthur. "My request is simple: I ask that you make this little friend I hold in my arms a Knight of the Round Table. I cannot tell you his name, but know that he is of very noble blood."

Her words were met with laughter, because it seemed quite ridiculous that such a hideous little creature should be knighted. The laughter quieted when, at the maiden's signal, three richly dressed squires entered the room. One was carrying a small sword and a small black shield, which bore three golden leopards with azure crowns. Another carried a small suit of armor with arabic designs, and a pair of golden spurs. The third held the reins of a spirited filly.

"What magical spell is this, Merlin?" murmured King Arthur. Instead of responding, the magician said, "Grant the favor that has been asked of you." So, although he was very uncertain, King Arthur knighted the dwarf and gave him the tiny sword. The dwarf behaved like a gentleman. He swore his fidelity to the king, said goodbye to all, and with the help of the maiden, he mounted his filly and rode off.

He had not gone ten miles in the forest when there appeared a knight who was riding a great fighting steed. As soon as the knight saw Bianna, he shouted, "Ah, I have searched for you forever, and finally I have found you. Come with me!" Bianna was very frightened and stopped in her tracks. The knighted dwarf came forward and said, "Sir, this maiden is under my protection so be on your way!" "Quiet, you ugly creature," responded the knight. The dwarf yelled, "I challenge you, villain!" He put his lance in position, took his shield in hand, and spurring his mount furiously, he charged his opponent.

As soon as he saw the dwarf coming, the knight burst out in scornful laughter, and raised his shield just slightly. But the dwarf's lance pierced him with such fury that it tore him from his saddle and flung him to the ground in a daze. The dwarf dismounted and with his sword pointed at the knight's neck, he shouted, "Ask forgiveness or you will die!" "Please forgive me!" the knight begged. "I shall. But under these conditions: you must go directly to King Arthur and declare yourself to be his prisoner and tell him that you were beaten by the dwarf whom he knighted not long ago."

"I swear that I will," said the knight. The dwarf-knight and the lovely Bianna began to ride again, and a few hours later a page at the castle of Camelot announced to King Arthur that a wounded knight was asking to speak with him. All were present and saw that his steel armor had been pierced by a lance. "Who are you, and who has wounded you?" the king questioned. "Ah, Sire," the good knight responded, "I am the son of noble King Avadean and I have been wounded by the dwarf who says that you knighted him." All of the knights were very surprised to hear this, and King Arthur murmured, "This is very strange. I wonder who that dwarf could be?" Then Merlin the Magician stepped forward and said in a very serious voice, "Know that that dwarf is the son of King Brangore d'Estrangore. Until not too long ago, he was the most handsome young man to be found in Great Britain and Brittany. A lovely damsel who was an expert magician fell in love with him, but he refused her love, because she was heartless and pitiless. To revenge herself, the damsel transformed him into the horrid dwarf that we all see."

THE DEPARTURE OF MERLIN

Almost the entire summer had passed, and the Knights of the Round Table had gone on many adventures in the name of King Arthur and Queen Guinevere. All were quite proud and very pleased, too.

Merlin the Magician, however, was very quiet and did not come down from his tower very often. Then one day he unexpectedly announced to good King Arthur and Queen Guinevere that he was going away. "This time, I have the feeling that I will not return." "Don't go, Merlin, I beg you!" cried the queen, her face turning pale. Merlin shook his head. "I cannot. It is written in the Book of Destiny that I will leave." Arthur and Guinevere insisted for quite a while, but in the end they had to give Merlin permission to leave.

So a few days later, he left Camelot. He left all by himself, on an autumn day, when the fog was as thick as it had ever been, and the yellow leaves fell quietly from the trees, one by one, like sorrowful rain.

THE ADVENTURES OF SIR GAWAINE

A year went by and Sir Gawaine presented himself to King Arthur, asking his permission to go in search of Merlin the Magician. The king gave him his blessing, and Sir Gawaine, followed by other knights, left Camelot. Then each knight took a different route and Sir Gawaine turned toward the cold lands of the north.

He traveled for days and days, and met only a few woodsmen and hermits. He asked each one if he had seen Merlin, but no one was able to tell him anything. He was galloping along, very sad, when he passed a damsel. He was so deep in thought that he did not see her, and did not say hello. The damsel stopped her horse, and exclaimed, "Sir Gawaine, they say that you are a great knight, but I see that you are instead a villain, with very bad manners." Embarrassed, Sir Gawaine responded, "You are right. Please forgive me."

"No, I shall not forgive you," exclaimed the damsel, insulted. "You shall be what you deserve to be: you will become just like the first man you see on your way." But Sir Gawaine did not give any weight to her threat, and responded, "You know my name, but I do not know yours." "Vivien," the damsel said, and she left.

Toward evening, he happened to meet some other travelers along the road. Approaching were the lovely Bianna and the dwarf-knight. Once again, Sir Gawaine was completely absorbed in his thoughts and he failed to recognize them. Nonetheless, he greeted them, saying, "God bless you!" "God save you, gentle knight," they responded. All of a sudden, the double spell was cast. The dwarf returned to a handsome young man, and Sir Gawaine became a deformed dwarf. His armor felt very large, and his helmet slipped around on his head. When he looked down from his horse, he felt as if he were on top of a very tall mountain!

Terrified, he let himself to the ground, and with great difficulty, took his armor off. "Ah," he exclaimed, "that damsel was a magician!" He left his horse, which was much too tall for him, and continued on his way, on foot.

THE PRISON OF AIR

Ah, how difficult it was for Sir Gawaine to roam about the forest in that condition! The few people that he did meet scorned him, laughed at him, and did not answer his questions. A country farmer even kicked him as he passed by. "Ah, poor me! I will never be able to find Merlin the Magician in the terrible state I am in! How could I win any battles? And how can I return to face King Arthur like this? Ah, how cruel we were to laugh at the dwarf-knight! I wonder who that damsel Vivien could be, to cast such a horrible spell on me?" And so he continued to roam the forests and plains searching in vain for Merlin the Magician.

He walked and walked until he ended up in a very beautiful forest. Suddenly, he heard a familiar voice calling him. He looked all around but did not see anyone. All he could see was a light mist just in front of him. He took a step forward and stopped. The mist was like a wall, and he could not pass through it. "What a mystery! I wonder what this could be?"

All of a sudden he recognized the voice and shouted, "Merlin, Merlin, is that you? Where are you?" "Ah, Gawaine, I am enclosed in a prison, much more solid than a tower of stone! I am locked in a prison of air, and I am sentenced to stay closed in here until my death!" "Whoever cast such a spell on you?" asked Sir Gawaine. "The maiden I love, and to whom I myself taught these magical spells!" "What is this cruel maiden's name?" "Vivien is her name. But now, tell me why and how you were transformed into a dwarf? If I were not a great magician myself, I certainly would not have recognized you at all!"

"Ah Merlin, the dame that transformed me into a dwarf is the same Vivien who has imprisoned you!" "How unwise it was of me to teach her my magical tricks! Now I am gone forever! No one can help me. Good bye, Sir Gawaine, good bye. Go back to Camelot! I love Vivien very much and prefer to remain her prisoner, than to live free and without her. Please tell King Arthur not to send anyone else to come and search for me. Give my greetings to the king and the queen and all of the Knights of the Round Table." These were the last words to pass from the lips of the legendary Merlin the Magician.

THE VILLAINOUS KNIGHTS

Sadder than ever, Sir Gawaine walked away from the prison of air, and left the splendid forest of Broceland. His misfortune had been very great: he had found Merlin, but he was not able to bring him back to Camelot, and he himself had been transformed into a deformed dwarf. Ah, Vivien was very cruel to have imprisoned the magician and to have transformed Sir Gawaine into such a horrible creature!

As he walked along, very tired and embittered, (imagine how difficult it was for him to make his way in such deep snow!) he suddenly heard a call for help. He ran ahead and saw two knights who had forced a sweet young maiden to dismount from her horse. They were holding her, and were about to steal all of her belongings. Sir Gawaine dashed ahead, forgetting that he was now a dwarf, and shouted, "Stop, villains! You are dishonoring that gentlewoman! Let the damsel go, immediately, or else!"

As he was saying these words, Sir Gawaine suddenly remembered the state he was in, and he became quiet. The two knights eyed him with scorn and asked, "Who are you, little runt?" "I am a Knight of the Round Table!" The two knights burst out laughing. "Ah, you are a knight! Well, mutant of nature, get out of here, or we will squash you like a little worm." Sir Gawaine was about to turn and leave when suddenly he remembered that when the son of King Brangore was a dwarf, he had had the courage to confront the son of King Avadean and to defeat him. "If he did it, I can do it too!" Sir Gawaine said to himself. Suddenly all of his courage returned. Taking his sword in both hands he attacked the two knights.

The knights did not expect to be charged and were trying to remove the damsel's necklace. His attack took

them by surprise. One knight fell to the ground unconscious, and the other took a great leap backward in fright, raising his sword into the air. But Gawaine was stronger than they were and certainly would have killed them both, if the damsel had not just then called out, "Oh, stop!"

"If you had not ordered me to stop," said Gawaine turning to the damsel, "I would have had no pity on such villains. They were not only villains, they called me a deformed dwarf, too!"

"And what do you think you are?"

asked the damsel with a cruel smile. Gawaine was in fact so excited by the duel that he forgot he had been transformed into a dwarf.

Hearing her words he let his sword drop, and he bowed his head in tears. "Come on, look at me," the damsel then said to him. Gawaine scornfully raised his gaze and . . . to his amazement, he realized that the damsel he had saved was the same Vivien who had transformed him into a dwarf ! Seeing her, he was unable to speak, but Vivien said, "I am grateful to you, Sir Gawaine. If I

were to give you back your true appearance, what would you give me in exchange?" "All that I possess in the world," responded Sir Gawaine. "I ask you to take two oaths. The first is that you always be courteous to damsels and greet them when you see them." "I swear," said Gawaine. Then Vivien added, "the second is that you will not search for Merlin ever again." "Ah, damsel, I certainly cannot swear to this, even if I must remain a deformed dwarf for the rest of my life!" Vivien smiled. "It is as I expected you would answer!" she said. Then she traced her magic symbols in the air and suddenly disappeared, and so did the two evil and villainous knights. Gawaine was transformed again into the strong and handsome knight he had always been, and right next to him appeared a magnificent steed. He mounted the steed right away and headed home toward Camelot, across the great forest.

THE RETURN OF SIR GAWAINE

After some time, he arrived at the castle, and he was both happy and sad at the same time. Happy because he was no longer a horrid dwarf; sad because he would have to tell King Arthur that Merlin the Magician was gone forever, destined to live the rest of his life in a prison of air, in which he had enclosed himself for the love of the beautiful and cruel Vivien.

When King Arthur was told Merlin's destiny, he shed many, many tears, and then he walked aimlessly alone in the forests that surrounded the castle. He also ordered that for ten days all should fast, that no one should drink any wine, and that all of the knights would attend mass every day, shoeless and without their swords.

Finally he called them to the Round Table and said to them:

"Gentlemen, let us all remember Merlin, and that God will welcome him in heaven when it is his turn. But above all let us remember all that Merlin said to us, and that it is our duty to search for and to find the Holy Grail." All of the knights then bowed their heads and prayed in silence.

Some years passed, and the Knights of the Round Table earned a glorious reputation with their adventures and their chivalry in battle, and King Arthur was renown throughout the world. Nothing, however, not even the sun, is without blemishes, and Arthur's blemish was not to have come to the aid of King Ban of Benwick, who was attacked by an enemy king and then died in battle while losing his kingdom. When Arthur heard this, he was remorseful and regretful and spent ten days in a monastery to do penitence.

THE YOUNG MAN WITH NO NAME

A few years went by, and one day, on the eve of Saint John's Day while Arthur was returning from the hunt, there appeared on the road to Camelot an extraordinary procession. It was extraordinary not simply because it was very extravagant, but also because it was all white. The horses were white, the knights' uniforms were white, and bright white were the veils that covered the dame leading the procession. White also was the regal uniform of the young man who rode directly behind her. King Arthur was quite marveled by all of this. He stopped and asked: "Oh damsel, who are you who shine and sparkle with such brilliance?" "God bless you, Sire. They call me the Lady of the Lake, and so you might call me as well. I have heard them speak of your Round Table and I bring you this young man, praying that you might accept him as one of your chivalrous knights. Know that he is the son of a king."

"I would accept him quite willingly," answered King Arthur. "What is his name?" "I cannot tell you, and he himself does not remember." "This is very strange, but we are living in a time of enchantments. Let us go to my castle." When they arrived at the castle, all admired the handsome young man in white, who, escorted by Sir Gawaine and Sir Dodinas le Savage, spent the night in prayer in the church of Saint Stephen. He was then knighted the

Many of the knights intervened, one at a time, and said, "It is true, you are too inexperienced for this feat in which you could lose your life."

The young man replied, "I must fight my first battle one day, and if I should die, King Arthur would not be sad because he would have lost an inexperienced knight. If instead one of you were to die, the king would have reason to mourn, having lost a knight of fame and experience." Hearing these words, all were quiet and Queen Guinevere exclaimed, "Well said! Sire, send this young man with no name, and whatever shall be, shall be!" "Very well, my friend, be on your way," said Arthur, "and return the victor." The young man kissed the king's cape and soon afterward, armed from head to foot, he left Camelot.

following morning, at the Feast of Saint John. The Lady of the Lake then bid farewell to the king, but before she left she said to the young man: "Console yourself, for now you are a knight and tomorrow you shall become famous. Soon you shall know what your name is. Remember me, for I have raised you like a son, and please remember something else: do not ever be afraid of anything."

"I shall do as you have ordered," said the young man and he kissed the Lady of the Lake's hand, bathing it with his tears. Then he returned to the hall of the Round Table and found much confusion. In fact, a message had arrived from the Princess of Nohant, an ally of King Arthur. The King of Northumberland had attacked her, and she was asking for the assistance of a knight who could save her. All of the knights asked to be chosen for this and King Arthur did not know how to decide. Then the young man with no name stepped forward and said: "Sire, send me." "You? If I am not mistaken, you have never fought a battle before."

THE TWO KNIGHTS

The knight with no name arrived some time later in the lands of the Princess Nohant. The country had been devastated and the villages burned. On the roads, there were groups of fearful peasants who did not know where to go. In the sky circled black storms of crows. The armies of the King of Northumberland were busy attacking the castle, so the knight was able to enter the city of Nohant with little difficulty. He presented himself to the princess and said: "Madam, King Arthur sends me to defend you." "God bless the king!" exclaimed the princess. "Tomorrow the enemy king will come to challenge me. What is your name?" "I am sorry, madam," responded the young man, "but this I cannot tell you." "And why not? You do not have a noble name?" "No, it is that I myself do not know what my name is."

Hearing these words, the princess got very upset and said, "Tell me at least which have been the battles that you have won." "None. I have never fought a battle."

The princess grew very pale and silent, but she said to herself: "How could King Arthur send me this inexperienced knight?" "Prepare yourself and pray, sir," she said to him, "because

tomorrow you must fight." "That I shall do, madam," responded the young man simply, and he retired. As the Princess Nohant cried sadly over her misfortune (in fact she was sure that the knight with no name would be killed by the champion of the King of Northumberland and he would therefore take over her city) it was announced to her that an errant knight was arriving at the castle.

Not long afterward a very tall, strong man with a handsome blond beard presented himself to the princess. "In your honor, madam," said the knight. "I am Sir Kay, step-brother and counselor to King Arthur. I was just returning to Camelot, and passing through your country I saw that it has been sacked and devastated. I come, therefore, to ask if you are in need of my help." "Ah, Sir Kay," exclaimed the princess "you are quite welcome!" And she told him how a knight with no name had arrived, saying he had been sent by King Arthur in person.

"I do not believe that at the Round Table there sits a knight with no name," said Sir Kay. "Let me see this young man: maybe he is an impostor or a madman." Sir Kay was then taken to the wing where the knight with no name was lodged and, after having said his name, he asked him, "And you, my sir, what is your name? Who are you?" "I do not know my name, but I know for certain that I am a Knight of the Round Table." "I have never seen you at that table."

"King Arthur knighted me just a few days ago and sent me here to defend Princess Nohant." "Do not worry about that: I am here and I will fight for her." "No, my sir, I have received my orders from the king and I shall carry them out!" replied the knight with no name.

Sir Kay answered him very brusquely, and the two knights might have drawn their swords, if the Princess Nohant had not arrived, saying: "In the name of God, do not argue. If I can have two champions, you shall both fight." Right in that very moment a trumpet was heard and a sound like thunder: the King of Northumberland had arrived with his army at the gates of the city.

THE BATTLE OF NOHANT

This king was a large man and very heavy, with a horrible tangled yellow beard and eyes like a hawk. He rode his horse right up to the gates of Nohant, followed by a knight dressed in black from head to toe.

"Princess!" he shouted, "send out the man who will fight mine!" From high, the princess responded, "I am sending out two champions instead of one."

The king gave a signal, and from his army a second knight came forward, this one dressed in black as well. "We are ready, Princess!" said the king. Then the doors of the city opened and Sir Kay and the knight with no name appeared, the first dressed in red, and the second in white.

Then a herald shouted, "When the trumpet will sound, the knights shall come forward: two against two; the battle will be decided from this encounter!" The four knights prepared themselves, with their lances ready, while the citizens of Nohant crowded around the walls of the city and watched with bated breath.

The princess shook with fear and thought: "All of my hopes are with Sir Kay, because the knight with no name will surely be beaten right away in the first encounter!"

Finally the sound of the trumpet was heard: the four knights lowered their lances and spurred their horses, and charged two against two. They met with such great force that their lances broke into a million shards, and pieces of armor fell here and there. Sir Kay hit his adversary very hard and threw him from his saddle, but he himself was hit very hard too, and fell. Instead,

the knight with no name knocked his adversary to the ground and remained firm in the saddle. From the walls of the city there suddenly arose a great shout of surprise and joy.

The battle (which was a real duel to the death) started again immediately. Sir Kay and his enemy drew their swords and began to attack. The knight with no name jumped swiftly to the ground, saying: "I shall never fight from horseback with a man on foot!" and he bared his sword. They engaged in battle and in a few minutes he was able to defeat his enemy, who asked for mercy and surrendered. Sir Kay instead had to fight very hard to win; and in the end he was battered and terribly bloody.

The inhabitants of Nohant applauded, the princess cried for joy and the King of Northumberland, seeing both of his champions on the ground, justly accepted the difficult defeat and departed with his armies. This is how the land of Nohant was saved.

SARAH AND THE THREE SHIELDS

Everyone gathered around the knight with no name and the Princess Nohant asked him to stay in Nohant. However, the young man said he must go, and went on to meet his destiny.

A few days later he reached the bank of a stream that bordered the country of Nohant, and hot from traveling, he dismounted and drank from the stream, and then sat under a tree to rest. He was sitting near a ford, at the shallowest part of the cool blue stream. Suddenly a knight came riding toward him, dressed in green with a steel helmet that hid his face. "Beware, do not cross the stream at that ford!" he shouted. But the knight with no name was not intimidated. "We'll see about that!" he answered. Jumping on to his horse, he rode toward his adversary and knocked him from the saddle, causing him to fall right into the river. When he fell, the knight lost his helmet

and suddenly long, shiny blond locks tumbled down, that framed the sweet face of young woman!

The knight with no name was stupefied and did not know what to say, but the young woman smiled at him and exclaimed, "Finally the one has arrived who will take the Dolorous Gard!" "I do not understand what you have said, damsel, but I am very sorry to have hit you," said the bewildered knight. "Oh no, I am quite happy for it. You must know that, beyond this river there is a castle that was once called the Joyous Gard. Then it was called the Dolorous Gard, because it was taken by an evil king, Brian of the Isles, who keeps all prisoner who live there, and who oppresses the farmers of the land. Only I was able to escape from the castle, and, dressed as a knight I positioned myself at this ford, waiting for a young man courageous enough to help me with the battle against the evil and powerful King Brian."

"You have not found anyone?" "No," responded the young woman, "until now, hearing my threats everyone has fled. But now I know that you will help me. My name is Sarah. What is your name?" "I have no name," responded the good knight.

Sarah then raised her hands to the sky and exclaimed, "The destiny is fulfilled! Here, in the castle there is a book of magical secrets, in which it is written that the knight who will save the Dolorous Gard will learn his name from this. Therefore, come with me." The young woman lead the knight to a cave, where they were greeted by valets who took the knight's armor, offered him food and drink, and took care of his horse. The young woman said to him: "You must know that the Dolorous Gard is protected by rings of walls, each one with a gate that is defended by ten villainous knights who will not fight you one by one, but all together. Do not fear, however, and

look at these." Sarah motioned to three silver-colored shields, the first with one red stripe, the second with two, and the third with three red stripes. "These shields," continued Sarah, "are quite magical: the first will add to your strength the strength of one man, the second that of two, and the third that of three men. Rest now, for tomorrow you must fight."

THE DOLOROUS GARD

The next morning, the knight with no name prayed devoutedly, then donned his armor and mounted his horse, and placed the shield with one stripe on his arm. He placed the shield with two stripes on his saddle. Then he rode toward the Dolorous Gard which rose spectacularly above a glistening lake. When he reached the walls of the tower, he sounded his horn. The evil King Brian of the Isles then appeared on the bastions and asked: "What do you want?" "I want you to free the castle." King Brian laughed and shouted: "Come here and we'll see!" Just then the door opened and ten knights appeared. Without saying a word they lowered their lances and rode together toward the knight with no name. Ten against one made for a very difficult battle! The knight was able to survive the first attack and went on to wound his enemies left and right. When he began to feel weak he threw down the first shield and picked up the second one. Suddenly his weariness faded and he was able to fight even more valorously than before. He became so strong that the last three knights put down their swords and surrendered for good.

Then the door to the castle magically opened once again. The knight with no name entered the first ring of walls and found the second ring, where there were ten more knights prepared to battle. "Wait my friend!" a voice said. It was Sarah who ran toward him, followed by valets. They gave him a fresh horse and a new helmet, and Sarah handed him the third shield with the three stripes. "Damsel," said the knight, "I shall be dishonored if I continue to fight with these enchanted shields." "Everything is enchanted here," answered the damsel. "Look up there, on the walls!" The young man looked up and saw that right above the door there was a copper statue of a giant, who held in his hand an enormous axe. The statue was made in such a way that the axe would fall on anyone who attacked the castle, if he only looked at the giant.

In fact, as soon as the young man looked straight into the eyes of the giant, the giant opened his hand and the axe fell. It happened to fall directly on the ten knights, injuring one of them and scaring the others away.

In that very moment the young man attacked his enemies, and was victorious. The door to the castle opened suddenly and all of the townspeople ran to meet the chivalrous knight and to congratulate him.

SIR LAUNCELOT DU LAKE

That evening, the young man said to Sarah: "Damsel, you told me that here I would discover my name." The young woman lead him to a cloister in the castle where there were many tombs. "Look at the headstones," said Sarah. The young man looked and suddenly found himself in front of a large marble slab on which was engraved: "Only the conqueror of the Dolorous Gard shall be able to open this tomb." Sarah then said: "King Brian attempted in vain to lift the slab. However, he was not the conqueror we have waited for; he was instead the usurper." The knight reached out and with no effort lifted the heavy marble slab. Hidden underneath was a tomb which read: "Here will lie Launcelot du Lake, son of King Ban of Benwick." And this was how the valorous knight discovered his name.

LAUNCELOT AT THE COURT OF KING ARTHUR

Launcelot returned to King Arthur in Camelot, where he was greeted with honor and seated among the Knights of the Round Table. He was respected immediately, not only because he was intelligent and generous, but also because he was undefeated with lance and spear. He won every tournament he entered. Everyone said: "Maybe he is the pure and fearless knight who will sit on the Seat Perilous and find the Holy Grail," but Launcelot did not think he deserved this honor.

If Launcelot was dauntless in the tournaments, he was even more valorous in battle. Since Launcelot had come to Camelot, King Arthur had fought many wars, against pagan invaders such as the Saxons, the Scots, and the Caledonians, and against kings who threatened the realm of Logris. In the wars, Launcelot always fought with great chivalry; so much so that in a short time he became almost as well-known as King Arthur himself. Queen Guinevere was one of Sir Launcelot's greatest admirers. She even called him the "jewel of the knighthood," and to show just how much she admired him, she gave him a beautiful ring that he never removed from his finger.

Everyone was a friend of Launcelot, but his closest friend was Gawaine even though he was a little bit older than Launcelot. Gawaine had never fought Launcelot in a tournament, and everyone asked, "If they were to duel, who would be the winner?" It was a question that seemed destined never to be answered; but alas, it was, and we shall see just when and how.

THE KIDNAPPING OF GAWAINE

One spring day, Gawaine, Launcelot, and the young Sir Galessin rode into the forest near Camelot. They were walking along without armor and without swords, and they sat down to talk in the shade of an oak tree. Suddenly, a huge knight burst out on to the field. He was so big that he looked like a giant. He rode toward the three men, and then turned to Gawaine and yelled, "Here is the traitor!" And before Gawaine could say one word, the knight grabbed him and slung him across the saddle, and disappeared quickly into the forest.

Galessin and Launcelot, unarmed as they were, could do nothing to help their friend. They returned quickly to the castle, armed themselves, and left in search of the knight. They soon found his tracks, but where two roads met the tracks disappeared. So the knights decided to split up: one went east and the other went west.

THE IMPRISONMENT OF GAWAINE

The giant knight led Gawaine to a large tower, which rose beyond the realm of Logris, in the middle of a large swamp. As soon as Gawaine entered the tower, a horrid and unkept woman shouted, "Gawaine, you will finally pay for your betrayal!" "On my honor," replied Gawaine, "I have never betrayed anyone in my life."

"You lie, villain: you killed my son! He was the bravest knight in the whole world, and so you could only have killed him by betrayal." The woman began to beat Gawaine until he bled. Then she yelled at the giant knight, "Carados, what are you waiting for? Throw him into the prison!"

It could hardly be called a prison. Gawaine was thrown into a deep well filled with snakes and teeming with insects. The serpents wound around his legs and bit him, while the insects climbed over his entire body.

A few days went by and Gawaine realized that he was destined to die a horrible death. He could hear no voices, and only a little bit of light entered his cell. The snakes and insects never stopped attacking him. Slowly he grew weaker and weaker, as he bled from his wounds and snake bites. "Oh my good King Arthur!" he thought, "and my dear friends of the Round Table, what a sad fate I have been given! I would have preferred to die in battle, in the service of the king and queen, when instead I must die here without knowing why, while serpents and earthworms feed on me!" He could not hold back his tears, and he wept, growing more and more tired as the hours passed.

MORGANA THE DISLOYAL

Launcelot continued his search. It was almost dawn, when he found himself in a clearing by a brook. On the bank, a dame sat crying unconsolably. All around her pieces of lances and bits of armor and blood-stained shields were scattered, along with two dead horses. They were sure signs that a battle had taken place. Seeing Launcelot, the woman rose to her feet and said, "Please, have pity on me!"

"Have no fear," responded the knight, smiling, as he dismounted his horse. "Why are you crying? What has happened here?" "Oh, sir, I am crying because the valets accompanying me have been attacked and wounded by an evil knight, who carries a golden shield with a green lion painted on it!"

"Was he alone?" Launcelot asked right away. "No. He was followed by a few pages, who brought along a bound man, and they beat him so viciously that he was bloody all over."

"Gawaine!" said Launcelot. "Do you know that evil knight?" "I had never seen him before, but I believe that he is Carados the Great of the Dolorous Tower." "Where is this tower?" "If you accompany me to my castle, I will tell you," said the dame.

Launcelot put himself at the dame's service and escorted her along a path through the forest, until they reached a small castle. The dame clapped her hands and the doors opened, and suddenly a few pages appeared, who ran quickly to her. "Prepare some good

wine right away for this knight, who was courteous enough to escort me. And you, sir, come with me. You must be tired, and will want to rest."

They entered the castle and a servant brought some wine in a crystal goblet. As soon as the wine had touched his lips, Launcelot fell into a deep sleep. The dame then ordered: "Take him straight to the prison."

That dame was Morgana le Fay, the sister of King Arthur, who was as beautiful as she was wicked. A student of Merlin the Magician, she had learned the art of magic from him; but instead of using it for good she used her spells to create evil. She was feared in all of Great Britain and beyond.

When she was in Camelot, Morgana lived in a tower of the castle, surrounded by damsels dressed in black and by her faithful servants. Often, however, she went and closed herself in a cave in the forest or in the castle where she had taken Launcelot (it was a secret castle of which no one knew the whereabouts), or she went for some time to the mysterious island of Avalon, an enchanted and magical isle.

She was envious of everyone, but especially of Queen Guinevere who was more beautiful, kinder, and more admired than Morgana. So Morgana had decided to harm her as much as possible, even at the cost of ruining the entire realm of Logris.

THE DOLOROUS TOWER

The next morning, Morgana awakened Launcelot and said to him: "If I had wanted to, I could have killed you. Now you are my prisoner, and I will not let you go until you give me the ring that the queen gave to you."
"Never!" replied Launcelot, and he added, "Who are you to know all of this?" He had never seen nor met Morgana le Fay. She answered, "Do not worry about that. Know instead that your friend Gawaine will never be freed." "How can you be so cruel?"
"I am not cruel, and to prove so I will come to a compromise with you: if I let you go you must promise to return to me as soon as you have freed the knight Gawaine." Launcelot was so anxious to help Gawaine that he promised. Morgana then called two pages who escorted him to the great swamp, from the middle of which the Dolorous Tower rose. Here they left him. "How shall I get in?" thought Launcelot as he surveyed the tower.
"I see no roads, and if I cross the great swamp, I should certainly sink right in together with my horse." Suddenly the door of the tower opened and Carados the Great appeared. Launcelot was quick to hide himself behind a tree, and from there he saw the knight ride his horse across the swamp, and into the forest. "I am sure that beneath this stagnant water there is a path of stones upon which a horse can walk with no danger!" thought Launcelot.
When Carados reached firm ground, Launcelot raised his lance and approaced him shouting, "Carados, you kidnapped Gawaine! Free him immediately, or I will kill you!" The giant knight turned around and saw him,

and responded, "Who are you, who dares to challenge me?" "I am Sir Launcelot du Lake!" "Well, this will be your last duel!" said Carados.
Then Carados threw himself against Launcelot. Their lances broke immediately, and then they fought with their swords. Carados was so strong that his sword sank two inches into Launcelot's helmet. He was not able to pull it out, so he turned his horse and fled toward the tower across the great swamp. Launcelot followed him. Then Carados shouted: "Open the door!"

He knew that if he were able to enter the tower he would be safe. Just as the giant was about to cross the threshold of his refuge, Launcelot took a great leap and grabbed Carados by the shoulders. Launcelot was able to enter the tower with him on his very horse.

Carados jumped to the ground and escaped up the stairs and along the walls of the tower. Launcelot followed him all the way. Suddenly, the giant leapt in to a moat that surrounded a small tower, which was Gawaine's prison. In the moat there was a small door that opened onto the snake pit. The malicious giant actually intended to kill his prisoner!

He moved toward the edge of the well and took a large boulder. He was about to throw it at the unhappy Gawaine when Launcelot grabbed him by the arm. A ferocious battle followed. Carados was much stronger and heavier than Launcelot, and once or twice he was about to smash him against the stone floor, or strangle him. But Launcelot was nimble, and always able to escape, and in the end with a well-planted blow, he pushed Carados down into the well, where he broke his neck in the fall and died.

Launcelot then went down into the well where he found Gawaine in a truly pitiful state. He lifted him up and carried him out to his horse, and they quickly left the Dolorous Tower. Half-way across the swamp the great tower suddenly tumbled down with a crash, and disappeared into the vast, limy waters of the swamp.

THE IMPRISONMENT OF SIR LAUNCELOT DU LAKE

In an abbey not far away, Gawaine was carefully tended to by the good friars and soon began to regain his strength. He thanked Launcelot for saving his life from a terrible end, and he said to him:

"Let us go back to Camelot. There I will tell everyone what you have done for me and you shall become even more famous." "Gawaine, my friend," said Launcelot, "I would come with you but I promised a dame whose name I do not know that I would return to her after I saved you. So go to Camelot alone and give my best wishes to the king and queen, and all of the knights. Very soon, I hope, I shall see you there." So the two knights separated: Gawaine went toward the castle of King Arthur and Launcelot toward the castle of Morgana le Fay. She greeted him very courteously when he arrived, saying: "I knew that you would return because

you are a man of your word." "Alas, lady, how long will you keep me prisoner here?" "Until you give me the ring that you wear on your finger." "Well, then I shall never leave this castle," sighed the knight.

Morgana smiled mysteriously. For some time after, Launcelot remained her prisoner: he was not chained, nor was he kept in a cellar; he was instead free to move about the castle, but he could not go near the doors, which were heavily guarded by armed valets. Against them the unarmed Launcelot would have been powerless.

"Well, if I cannot flee then I shall die here," Launcelot said to himself, "because I will never give the ring the queen gave to me to this cruel woman."

Fearing poison, Launcelot did not drink any wine. Morgana knew many tricks, however, and seeing that the knight had decided to resist, she put a few drops of poison on the bread he ate every evening. He fell into a deep sleep, and she took the ring from his finger and replaced it with a ring that was almost identical.

However, on the real ring, a very small knight and dame holding a heart were depicted. But they were very small, and unless the two rings were compared side by side no one would have been able to tell them apart.

When Launcelot woke up, he saw the ring on his finger and suspected nothing. With a sigh, he resigned himself to his lifelong imprisonment.

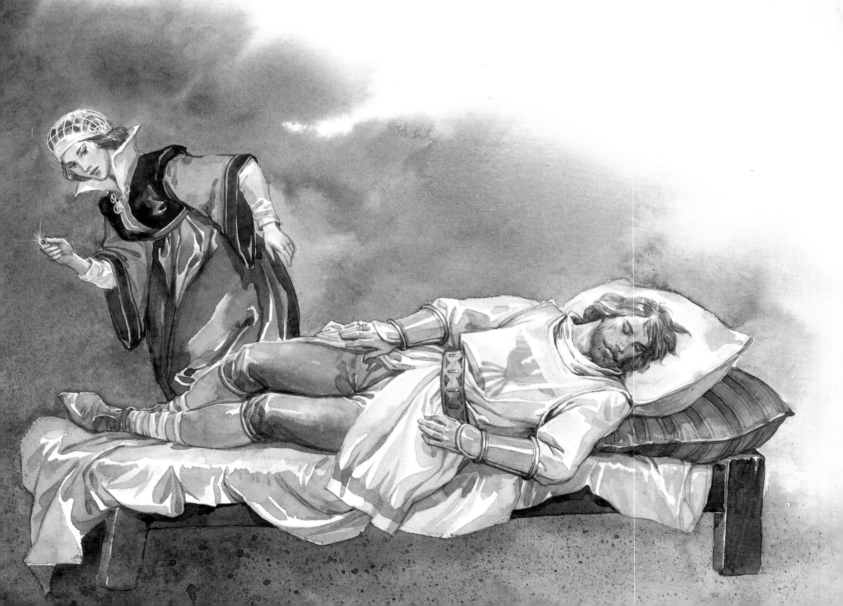

THE UGLY MAIDEN

Some time later, a maiden presented herself to King Arthur. She was the ugliest maiden that anyone in the castle had ever seen. "Sire," said the ugly maiden, "Sir Launcelot du Lake has sent me." Then she pulled the ring out of a small bag and threw it at the feet of the queen. "Here is the ring you gave to him: Sir Launcelot du Lake refuses it and says that he will never set foot in Camelot again!"
All of the knights rose to their feet in anger and Queen Guinevere let out a cry of pain. Sir Galessin picked up the ring and exclaimed: "It is impossible that Sir Launcelot could have wanted to offend the queen with such villainy!"
"Believe as you wish," responded the ugly maiden. Then she left.

The queen was unable to hold back her tears. King Arthur ordered that the woman be followed and brought back to the castle. But the valets who set off after her met Morgana le Fay instead, who was riding a black donkey toward Camelot. They asked her if she had seen the ugly maiden pass by, and she sent them in the opposite direction.
"We will find her!" shouted the valets as they rode on. Morgana smiled maliciously and murmured, "You will never find her!" The ugly maiden was in fact, Morgana herself, who had mischievously used one of her magical spells to change her appearance.

THE RETURN OF LAUNCELOT

The Knights of the Round Table would not believe for an instant that Sir Launcelot could have offended the queen, and they asked permission to go in search of their friend. Quite a few of them left, and a disturbing silence fell on the castle of Camelot. The lovely smile had disappeared from Queen Guinevere's lips and this event filled Morgana with evil joy.

She had forgotten, however, that some-one was protecting Launcelot: the Lady of the Lake. Her magical powers were stronger than Morgana's. So it happened that the Lady of the Lake had a dream in which she saw her favorite knight crying desolately. She asked the stars what had happened, and soon set out to find Launcelot. A dragon suddenly appeared before her and blocked the road. It was a horrible monster covered with shiny scales and had a frightening tail. The Lady of the Lake raised her hands above her head

and shouted: "Be gone, Morgana! You know that you are not stronger than I!" The dragon disappeared instantly, having been only an illusion created by Morgana le Fay.

Soon after, the Lady of the Lake was told by her valets that ten lions had appeared on a nearby hilltop. Again the Lady of the Lake raised her hands and shouted, "Be gone, Morgana! Out of my way!" The lions disappeared instantly. When the Lady of the Lake finally reached the castle, the door was open, and there stood Morgana in the doorway, dressed in black.

The two women looked at each other in silence. Then the Lady of the Lake said: "Free my son, Launcelot. You know that I am stronger than you are. I could lock you forever in a prison of air and I will do it, if you do not obey." When she was angry the Lady of the Lake seemed to shimmer like red-hot iron. Morgana was frightened and she kneeled down and said, "I surrender, Lady of the Lake, on one condition: that you tell no one that Launcelot was kept as my prisoner."

When Launcelot saw the Lady of the Lake, tears of joy came to his eyes, and he kneeled before her and kissed her gown. She said to him: "Go straight to Camelot, my son, but do not say who has kept you prisoner. Tell them instead that you were captured by pagan barbarians." And she added, "The stars have told me that you will suffer." "All men suffer," murmured Launcelot. "Yes. But you shall see the end of the Round Table, of the valorous

adventures, and all of this enchantment; for this you will suffer very much. On the other hand, everything must come to an end." Hearing these words, Launcelot became very sad. He mounted his horse and returned to Camelot. Only when he arrived did he realize that he was not wearing the ring Queen Guinevere had given him. He knelt before the queen and she gave him his ring back, and he swore that no one would ever remove it again.

From that day on, happiness and joy were restored to the castle, among the dames of the court and the Knights of the Round Table.

THE GLORY OF KING ARTHUR

The Knights of the Round Table, in those years, fought many wars in the name of King Arthur and earned much glory. But many of them, in search of the Holy Grail, lost their lives and did not return. So many did not return that at times there were very few knights seated at the Round Table. The knights asked themselves, "Will one of us be able to find the Holy Grail? And who will sit in the Seat Perilous?"

One day a knight named Moses dared to sit in the Seat Perilous: he was immediately struck down by lightning. There was, among the Knights of the Round Table, also a certain Sir Mordred who was the only nephew of King Arthur. He hoped to succeed King Arthur on the throne after his death. Mordred was a thin young man, very pale and always taciturn. He was valorous in battle, but cruel. Not many of the knights were fond of him, and many feared him because he was untrustworthy and ambitious. But we will learn more about him soon. Some time went by, and the glory and the power of King Arthur continued to grow as he became older. His beard and his hair, once blond, were now long, white and flowing. He had remained as strong and as chivalrous as he was in his youth, and to this he had added the wisdom that comes with age. King Arthur was revered in all the western hemisphere. Queen Guinevere had grown older too, but she remained as beautiful as ever, and it seemed that the wings of time had left her untouched, as if by magic.

THE CONSPIRACY

In the meantime, Morgana le Fay had not resigned herself to defeat, and she burned with the desire to discredit Queen Guinevere, whom she hated and envied more than ever. Envy is a horrible feeling; it can be seen through the eyes of men. Morgana, who knew just how to read a person's eyes, saw that just as she was envious of Queen Guinevere, so Sir Mordred was envious of King Arthur.

Inventing an excuse, she called the young man to her chambers and said to him: "Ah, Sir Mordred, I have read some news of your future in one of the ancient books that the magician left to me." Mordred asked quickly:
"What have you found out, madam?"

"That you shall never be the King of Logris." Becoming pale, Mordred said: "And yet, I am the king's heir!"
"Yes, but not the queen's, and she will attempt to put one of her family on the throne. Beware of Queen Guinevere my friend!" "But what can I do?"
"If you really want to know," whispered Morgana, "just listen to me." And she revealed her terrible plan to Mordred. As envy is the mother of hate, fear is the mother of every crime. Mordred was so envious of King Arthur and was so afraid that he would not become king, that when Morgana revealed her plan, he said:
"I am on your side, and I shall do as you say!" Thus the conspiracy that would destroy the kingdom of Logris and the Round Table was formed.

THE POISONED APPLE

Morgana le Fay waited for a time when Sir Launcelot and Sir Gawaine were away from Camelot, the former to battle a band of Vikings and the latter in exploration of a great forest. Then she poisoned, with a rapid and deadly poison, a beautiful apple and placed it in the fruit basket that was put on the Round Table. This was where the knights sat down to lunch every day. Morgana then thought to herself: "From evil, evil comes; something is bound to happen."

In fact something did happen. Queen Guinevere, who was happily seated with the knights, noticed the beautiful apple, and she reached out to take it. But when she saw young Sir Gaheris seated next to her, she said to him, "Please take this beautiful apple. I offer it to you as a sign of friendship." "As a sign of friendship I shall eat it," responded the knight. He took a bite out of the apple and grew very pale, rolled his eyes to the heavens, and fell to the floor with a sigh.

After the first fearful moments, everyone ran to his aid, but they realized immediately that he was dead.

The queen stuttered: "But what has happened?" No one dared to say anything, but evil Mordred (following Morgana's orders) said:

"We have all seen, madam. You have poisoned Sir Gaheris!" "How can you say such a thing?" exclaimed the queen. Mordred replied: "I call all who are seated around this royal table as my witnesses that you have given to Sir Gaheris an apple, and that he fell to the ground dead as soon as he bit into it." Everyone was silent, because this was actually the way it had happened. Certainly, if Sir Launcelot had been present, he would have taken the queen's defense, and no one would have ever dared to contradict him. If Sir Gawaine had been present he would have been able to calm everyone with his influence. But the two knights were not there, and Mordred hurried out of the room and ran to King Arthur and said: "Sire, a great misfortune has fallen upon you. The queen, your wife, has poisoned Sir Gaheris."

"This I cannot believe!" exclaimed King Arthur. He rushed to the great hall where he found everyone in silence. A few minutes later Sir Mador de la Porte returned from a mission in the north. He was the brother of Sir Gaheris. Mordred said immediately to him: "Ah, Sir Mador, what a tragedy for your good family! The queen has poisoned Sir Gaheris!" His face became as white as chalk, and Sir Mador said: "This cannot be!" But he soon realized that everyone was silent with anguish, and he lowered his eyes and saw Gaheris lying dead on the floor. He fell to his knees beside him, and crying desperately, he asked the other knights what had happened.

When he discovered that the queen actually had given the apple to Gaheris, he turned to her impetuously and said: "You handed him his death!"

"For the love of God," responded Queen Guinevere, terrified, "if I had known the apple was poisoned I would not have given it to anyone!"

"And yet you gave it to him! This was very cruel!" Then, Sir Mador turned to King Arthur and shouted: "Sire, the queen has killed Sir Gaheris by treason, and if she wishes to deny this, I am ready to prove it with my lance and spear! I will prove her guilt in battle!"

No king, not even King Arthur, with all of his glory and his power, could refuse this request. Queen Guinevere looked about, expecting one of the knights to come to her defense against Sir Mador de la Porte; but everyone was very frightened, and avoided her glance and kept his head down.

Overcoming her anguish, the queen said, "My king, what shall you decide?" King Arthur responded gravely:

"If you declare your guilt, my lady, death awaits you. If instead you declare your innocence, within ten days you must find a challenger who will prove your innocence in a duel with Sir Mador de la Porte."

The queen stood up, and solemnly proclaimed: "In the name of God, I am innocent." Then she turned, and, followed by her faithful attendants, she retired to her chambers.

THE TOURNAMENT AT CAMELOT

Many days went by. A few of the Knights of the Round Table who had gone away to fight wars or to search for the Holy Grail returned to Camelot and were told what had happened. The knights told them how Queen Guinevere had been accused of killing Sir Gaheris and how she must now wait for a champion who would defend her innocence. No one, however, stepped forward to put his lance and sword at her disposition because Sir Gaheris had been a good friend to all, and no one accepted the unfair way in which he had been killed.

Day by day the queen grew more and more upset, and asked herself many times: "Will I simply die without one single knight coming to my aid?" And she cried together with her attendants. One of them tried to console her by saying: "My queen, Sir Gawaine and Sir Launcelot are sure to help you, you shall see!" But the queen replied: "Alas, Sir Gaheris was the cousin of Sir Gawaine and how could he, even though he cares for me, aid someone who even unintentionally caused the death of one of his relatives? As for Launcelot, certainly he cares for me, but the Vikings are mighty warriors and who knows when he will be able to win the war and come home? Oh," continued the queen who was by now in tears, "if I only knew where he was now! I would send word to return right away!" But no one knew exactly where Launcelot and the knights that were accompanying him had gone.

The days went by, and preparations began for the large arena where the tournament would be held. It was the tournament that would decide the fate of Queen Guinevere. From all over the realms of Logris and Great Britain, kings, barons and knights arrived but no one stepped forward and offered his services to the queen. King Arthur was very sad, and seemed to have aged one-hundred years. He was a little relieved when Gawaine returned. He told him everything, and then asked: "Gawaine, my friend, will you let the queen be taken to the stake?"

"Sir, my heart is heavy, but she gave my cousin the poisoned apple. How could I defend her against my family? I would do it but only upon your orders." "This I would never ask you to do," murmured the king.

The day of the tournament finally arrived. The good people of Camelot crowded around the field, but it was different this time. No songs or applause were heard. The first encounters between the knights began; all eyes were fixed on Sir Mador de la Porte who stood in front of his tent, surrounded by his squires. No one dared to accept the challenge.

It was late afternoon when a knight arrived in Camelot. He seemed to have traveled very far. He rode alone, without a squire, and there was no coat of arms on his silver shield, which was instead painted with three red bands. He slowly went to the tournament field, where he presented himself to King Arthur. Without removing his helmet, he asked: "I have heard that today Queen Guinevere is being judged, because supposedly she has been accused of murder and betrayal. What wind of folly blows upon the realm of Logris, sire?"

Sir Mador overheard this, and exclaimed, "Knight, whoever you are, know that I am here to sustain that Queen Guinevere acted with disloyalty and betrayal." "And I am here to defend her," responded the unidentified knight. "I will prove that the queen is innocent!" So, at the last minute, Guinevere had found a challenger to defend her. Everyone was really very pleased, as was King Arthur. Gawaine was also happy, for although he had lost a cousin, he felt very loyal to his queen. Just then the trumpets sounded and the heralds announced the beginning of the duel for justice. If Sir Mador should win, the queen would be found guilty and condemned to the stake. If the other knight (whose name they still did not know) should win, the queen would be proven innocent.

There was complete silence as the two knights took their places on the field. Everyone looked on anxiously, and Queen Guinevere held her hands clasped tightly to her bosom. Her fate was about to be decided.

When Sir Kay the Seneschal gave the signal, the two knights lowered their lances, spurred their horses, and charged at one another. There was a great clash. Sir Mador was thrown from his saddle and fell to the ground, while his challenger dismounted right away with his sword in hand.

Sir Mador did not even have a chance to defend himself; his challenger wounded him immediately and pinned him to the ground. Placing his sword at Sir Mador's throat, the knight said: "Mador, you can see that you cannot win. Take back your accusations against the queen, or you shall die."

"Only one knight could have conquered me so quickly," replied Sir Mador, "and then act so generously. Just one knight: and you must be that knight. I take back the accusations that I unjustly made against the queen."

Returning to the king's stand, the knight announced that Sir Mador de la Porte had been defeated. As he took off his helmet, everyone immediately recognized him as Sir Launcelot.

At first there was silence, and then everyone began to shout with joy because Queen Guinevere had been saved, and Sir Launcelot du Lake had returned to Camelot.

MORGANA LE FAY'S SCHEMES

Sadder and more deluded than ever were Morgana and Mordred, who saw all of their plans go up in smoke. They met again and came up with a new, more terrible plot. "Listen to me, Sir Mordred," said Morgana. "You must go to the king and tell him that Queen Guinevere wants to kill him and marry Sir Launcelot. This way she would still be queen and Launcelot would be king." Sir Mordred said: "King Arthur will never believe me!" "And instead he will believe you, if you tell him that Guinevere wants to kill him in his sleep by placing a drop of poison between his lips. Tell him to look under the queen's pillow this evening before he retires," and she showed Mordred a small vial. "This contains a very potent and deadly poison. I will hide it under Guinevere's pillow. The king will find it there, and he will believe your story."

And so it happened. That evening when the king found the vial of poison under the queen's pillow, he was very, very surprised and he exclaimed, "Ah, Guinevere, I see that you are an expert with poisons. So it is true; you did poison the apple that killed Sir Gaheris! And now you want to do away with me, too, and give the crown to Launcelot!" The queen was shocked and replied, "Sire, I have no idea what you are

talking about! I know nothing about poisons!" But the king did not believe her and ordered that she be arrested and locked up in a tower to await her trial. He also ordered Sir Launcelot to be arrested. That evening the queen was taken away, as the moon shone brightly. The knights escorting her were crossing the town when suddenly the sound of hoofbeats was heard, and the clash of swords. The knights turned to see who was there. "Ho!" they shouted. "Who goes there?"
More knights then appeared, and one of them spoke: "I am Sir Launcelot du Lake! Let Queen Guinevere go!"
In fact, one of the servants in the castle had run to tell Launcelot what had happened to the queen. Launcelot had quickly gathered his friends and companions who were most faithful.
Sir Gaheriet said to Launcelot:
"We must obey the king's orders for your arrest, Sir Launcelot. Hand over your lance and sword!" "Come and get them!" replied Sir Launcelot, as he stepped forward. Perhaps he did not intend to cause a fight, no one could tell, but all of a sudden the battle began. Suddenly all of the knights who had up until that day behaved as brothers raised their swords against one another. At the sight of such a brawl, Mordred and his companions fled, abandoning the cart upon which the queen sat, bound, terrified and crying.

Table, and among them his beloved brothers. As soon as he saw them, he shed angry tears of mourning for his dear brothers.

"Cursed be Sir Launcelot du Lake!" he cried. "I renounce my friendship with him and swear that I will fight him until I have avenged my brothers!"

King Arthur came out to the square as well, and he ordered the fallen knights to be taken away. He immediately called a meeting of the Knights of the Round Table. Never had such a sad

THE WAR BETWEEN BROTHERS

Sir Mordred was the first to arrive at the castle, and he went quickly upstairs and presented himself to King Arthur. He was still covered with sweat and blood as he said: "Sire, Launcelot and his companions attacked us, and they have escaped with the queen!" Sir Gawaine, who was seated next to the king, shrugged and said, "Well done." Mordred turned to him and said: "Quiet! Even your brothers, Guerrehes and Gaheriet have been killed!" Beside himself with anger, Gawaine grabbed Mordred by the throat. "You lie!" he shouted at Mordred. But Mordred simply responded, "Go out to the square, Sir Gawaine, and see for yourself whether or not I am lying!" So Gawaine ran out to the square and there (oh, what a horrible sight!) lay many of the Knights of the Round

64

assembly been seen in the castle! Of the one hundred and fifty original knights, not more than sixty were present. Thirty-two had sided with the queen and Sir Launcelot; the others had all been killed. With tears welling in his eyes, King Arthur was unable to speak. Sir Gawaine spoke instead, saying, "Sir Launcelot has not only killed two of my brothers and other Knights of the Round Table, he has also disobeyed the king by setting the queen free. In the face of such rebellion, we must declare war on him!" Sir Kay said very sternly, "Gentlemen, this will be the end of the Round Table." Sir Mador de la Porte said: "A squire told me that Launcelot, his followers, and the queen are headed to the Joyous Gard, to lock themselves in the castle there." No one said anything, because they all knew that it was impossible to take the Joyous Gard. But seeing that the war had been decided, King Arthur said: "My armies will leave tomorrow for the Joyous Gard, and all of you shall ride with me."

THE ATTACK
ON THE JOYOUS GARD

In the meantime, Launcelot had called all of his faithful followers in Great Britain, and had sent messengers beyond the sea to Brittany, and to the realms of Benwick and Ganis, so that those castles were fortified for war, too.

A few days later, King Arthur's troops arrived at the Joyous Gard, ready to lay siege on the castle. Shelters, trenches and pavilions were prepared. King Arthur was holding counsel with his knights when it was announced that a damsel wanted to speak with him. The king said: "Show her in." The damsel stepped forward and said: "Sire, the knight Sir Launcelot du Lake sends me, and he has asked me to tell you that this war is not right:

Sir Gawaine's brothers were killed in battle, and the queen is innocent. He therefore asks for peace."

"There will not be peace!" shouted Gawaine as soon as the damsel had finished. "Go right now, and tell Sir Launcelot that there will never be peace between us!" The young woman answered: "So be it. But Merlin the Magician, who taught me his magical spells, told me that the descendant of King Ban of Benwick would never know defeat! My name is Vivien," she continued, looking straight into Gawaine's eyes, "and you should remember me, Sir Gawaine!"

And then she turned and left.

King Arthur asked Gawaine: "What did that damsel mean?" Sir Gawaine, who was quite disturbed, did not tell the truth, and said: "I do not know." But he remembered having been turned into a dwarf, and he had a disturbing premonition of misadventure.

The next day, the war began at the Joyous Gard. There were very bloody battles, and both sides lost many knights. King Arthur's armies, however, suffered even more. Despite Sir Gawaine's valor, Sir Ector, Sir Lionel and Sir Bohor were once able to reach King Arthur's tent, and they destroyed it. Another time, as he was battling the king but did not recognize him, Launcelot flipped the king from his saddle with a stroke of his sword, and the king fell to the ground.

"Launcelot, take that man's head, and we will have won the war!" shouted Sir Ector. Launcelot then realized that he had disarmed King Arthur. He got off of his horse and put King Arthur back into his saddle. Then he said, "Sire, next time, be on your guard."

THE RETURN OF GUINEVERE

Two months went by and the armies of King Arthur grew weak as they battled at the Joyous Gard. Queen Guinevere, pale and thin, asked to be returned to King Arthur on the condition that she would be freed of the accusations against her. And so Sir Launcelot came out of the Joyous Gard followed by the queen dressed in white. To King Arthur, Launcelot said, "Sire, here is your queen! If I had not helped her, she would have been killed even though she was innocent. I ask you to free her from the accusations and to receive her as a queen deserves."

The king, who was very moved, em-braced his queen. He was about to abandon the siege, when Sir Gawaine exclaimed, "We will go only if you, Launcelot, shall leave Great Britain for good. Know that wherever you may go, you shall have no peace." "Gawaine, may God watch over you," responded noble Sir Launcelot.

He sorrowfully returned to the Joyous Gard, and retired to the chapel where he prayed all through the night. Then he ordered one of his squires to take his shield to Camelot, and hang it in the church of Saint Stephen. He said, "I will never see that city again, nor the church where I was knighted, nor the queen I have so honored!"

The next day, Sir Launcelot mounted his horse, rode to the coast, and boarded a ship for Brittany. He was very sad, and as the shore grew farther and farther away, he said, "Oh sweet land, may God bless you. My heart and soul are forever with you!"

A few days later, Launcelot arrived in Brittany, and was crowned King of Ganis and Benwick. Many knights and barons swore their fidelity to him. He said: "I shall soon test your loyalty in the war." In fact, Sir Gawaine, in the end, had been able to convince King Arthur to wage war on Launcelot. They had a strong army, and had gathered an imposing fleet to attack the cities of Benwick and Ganis. As for the realm of Logris, King Arthur took the advice of Morgana le Fay, and left it in the hands of Sir Mordred. Alas! King Arthur did not know into what traitor's hands he had placed his realm! As Queen Guinevere said good by to Arthur, she added: "My dear husband, may God bless you and protect you. For some reason I am afraid that I will never see you again." The fleet sailed and after some time reached the shores of Brittany, in the realm of Ganis. Gawaine said, "Let's attack the city of Ganis, and then we shall destroy it!"

All of the barons agreed. But they were still talking when Launcelot's army attacked them by surprise. For two days they battled between land and sea, and once again brother laid hand on brother until King Arthur, filled with anguish, asked for a truce. He sent for Sir Launcelot. Sir Launcelot arrived, still covered with blood and dust, and asked, "What do you want, sire?"

King Arthur was silent, and Gawaine immediately exclaimed, "Launcelot, traitor and assassin, we wish to end this war with a duel. Do you accept?"

"I do. Who will be your challenger?"

"I will!" shouted Sir Gawaine.

Sir Launcelot replied, "And I shall be the challenger for my kingdom. Until tomorrow!" No one dared to speak, because the greatest knights of the Round Table who had been as close as brothers, were to battle until death.

THE DUEL

The duel took place a few days later, on a great open space beside the sea. All of the barons of Great Britain and Brittany were present, along with King Arthur. But never had anyone seen such a great but sad gathering of knights. No one talked, and everyone kept his eyes to the ground. Pain and anguish were in the hearts of all of the knights. Sir Gawaine or Sir Launcelot? One of them would die! What a horrible event for the knighthood!

Sir Launcelot arrived dressed in white, and Gawaine dressed in green. They were both armed from head to foot, and rode great steeds. At the sound of the trumpets, they charged. As the two knights battled, lances flew, and men and horses fell to the ground, and got right back up again. They drew their swords and injured one another again and again. And when their swords had broken in two, they continued to battle with wooden clubs.

Their armor broke into bits, their helmets were dented and blood flowed in all directions. The onlookers were terrified to silence; they shouted out just once as Gawaine was struck down by Sir Launcelot and remained on his knees, unable to stand. Sir Launcelot said, "Gawaine, my brother, this is enough." "No!" replied Gawaine, as blood flowed from his nose and mouth. "One of us must die!" And they began to fight again, but Sir Launcelot knocked Gawaine to the ground again. This time he went to King Arthur who was watching anxiously from his throne, and said: "Sire, order Sir Gawaine to withdraw, because if we continue the battle he will surely die."

"God bless you for your generosity, Sir Launcelot, but Sir Gawaine shall do as he wishes. If you want, you can with-

draw instead." "I will, because I have
always obeyed you," answered Sir
Launcelot, and he left. Sir Ector said to
him, "What are you doing? If you kill
Gawaine, you will have won the war."
"No, Ector, I would prefer to be stabbed
in the heart, rather than kill a man
who cannot defend himself."

MORDRED THE TRAITOR

When he returned to the city of Ganis, Sir Launcelot was cured by his doctors, who were amazed that he had not died from his numerous wounds. They congratulated him on his strength. Sir Gawaine's doctors, on the other hand, had more to worry about. They realized that he would not live much longer. Gawaine had lost his senses again, and knew nothing of what was going on around him.

A small sailboat had landed in the meantime, and a messenger came ashore, asking to be taken directly to King Arthur. When he was in front of the king, he kneeled and said: "Ah sire, what a terrible tragedy. Your nephew Mordred has crowned himself King of Logris, and has asked all of the bishops and barons to swear their fidelity to him." "And the queen?" asked King Arthur. "She has escaped to the Joyous Gard, where she has been beseiged and evil Sir Mordred has truthfully sworn he will have her beheaded!"

"That bloodthirsty villain!" shouted King Arthur, as he suddenly became aggressive again. Then he ordered his knights to sail back to Logris right away. And so the war against Sir Launcelot ended, and King Arthur left the realms of Ganis and Brittany.

THE DEATH OF SIR GAWAINE

Sir Gawaine came to his senses again when they were on the high seas. He looked about, his face as white as chalk, and asked, "Where are we?" "We are at sea, Gawaine," answered King Arthur, who had come immediately to his bedside. "We are going home, because Mordred has betrayed me and crowned himself King of Logris; he has even asked that all of the bishops and barons swear their fidelity to him." "Sire, how I suffer to be at the end of my life!" murmured Sir Gawaine. "I wish I could still go to battle for you, but, as you can see, I cannot."

Sir Gawaine was silent and then, with a long sigh, he continued: "Ah, it was a folly to battle Launcelot. Now, as all men who are about to die, I can see clearly: Launcelot never betrayed anyone. Send word to him that I am bitterly sorry to have insulted him, and that I proclaim him to be the most loyal knight in all of the kingdom. Ask Launcelot to help you, my king, and defend your crown!" And having said this, poor Sir Gawaine died.

At that moment, as if it were crying too, the sky grew dark and overcast, the clouds opened up and a thick and silent rain fell. King Arthur cried for a long, long time during the night. Everything that had happened lately meant just one thing: that the era of great adventures and enchantment was really coming to an end.

THE BATTLE OF SALISBURY

When Sir Mordred found out that King Arthur had left Brittany and was returning to Camelot, he was frightened and ran to Morgana to ask her advice. She then said to him: "Take Guinevere hostage immediately. Then ask the pagan Saxons for help, and meet King Arthur with your armies as soon as he lands. This way the reinforcements will not have time to reach him before you do."

Mordred followed her advice, and began moving toward the coast. He reached his destination just as King Arthur landed. Mordred had twice as

many soldiers and knights, and he lined them up ten deep. But King Arthur did not lose hope. He rode at the head of his army, and as he drew his glorious sword Excalibur, he gave the call to charge the enemy. The battle that followed was one of the greatest there had ever been. The ground quickly grew red with blood. One minute seemed as if King Arthur was winning, and the next, Mordred. From the boats came more of King Arthur's soldiers, as the Saxons attacked from the hills. The battle wore on, and the sky began to glow red, as if bloody from the battle as well.

Then came the clash of the arrays that escorted the two adversaries. When King Arthur saw his nephew the traitor, he attacked him, shouting threats and speeding toward him through the armies like a bullet. Mordred did not flee; instead it was he who struck first. Brave King Arthur remained in the saddle despite his age, and fought back. The battle was so difficult that only four of the original Knights of the Round Table remained: Sir Kay, Sir Dodinas le Savage, Sir Griflet le fise de Dieu and Sir Lucan the Butler. But they were all wounded, Dodinas more severly than the others.

Dodinas attacked Mordred, but was beheaded. Then Sir Kay came forward, but he was killed as well. "My goodness, how can you let Sir Kay be killed like this?" shouted King Arthur. He killed the Saxon, grabbed his lance, and charged Mordred. He pierced him many times with his sword. But before he died, Mordred found the strength to wield his own sword, and he struck King Arthur square in the chest.

The remaining knights, Sir Griflet le fise de Dieu and Sir Lucan the Butler, seeing King Arthur fall injured, raised their swords and attacked. They killed all of the followers of Mordred, but during the battle the remaining followers of King Arthur died as well.

THE DEATH OF KING ARTHUR

On the great plain, between the sea and the hills, there lay nothing but dead knights and horses. Sir Griflet and Sir Lucan began to search for their king, but to their surprise they did not find him dead on the ground, but seated on a large stone. Sir Griflet said, "Sire, are you all right?" "I am about to die," responded Arthur. "But I do not want to die here. Take me near to the sea." The two knights put their king on a horse and walked slowly next to him, (for they were very weak and tired as well) until they reached a chapel by the sea. Here Sir Lucan died for his many wounds, and King Arthur began to

pray for him. "To the sea," he then said. There, with great difficulty, he unsheathed Excalibur which was red with blood, and said, "Sir Griflet, take my sword and go beyond that hill. There you will find a lake. Throw Excalibur into the lake and then come back." "I will do that, my king," said the knight. He walked beyond the hill. There he found a tranquil lake. He was about to throw Excalibur into the lake, but he did not have the courage, and he threw his own sword into the lake instead. Then he returned to King Arthur, who said, "Have you obeyed me?" "Yes," replied Sir Griflet. "And what happened?" "The sword sank into the water." "Ah, Griflet, I am about to die, and you do not tell me the truth. Go back, and do as I said."

The knight returned to the lake, but again he did not have the courage to throw Excalibur into the water, and instead he threw in the sheath. He went back to the king, who said, "Have you obeyed me? What did you see?" "Nothing. The sword sank into the water. What should I have seen, my king?" "Griflet, Griflet, you are fooling with a dying man. Go back, and obey." Sir Griflet went back to the lake, and this time he did as King Arthur had asked him. What a miracle! Just as Excalibur was about to touch the water, a hand came up out of the lake and grabbed it, and, brandishing it three times, disappeared back into the lake. Griflet returned and told King Arthur what had happened. King Arthur smiled and said, "Now Sir Griflet, go on ahead and let me die." The knight obeyed and left crying. He was not far from the beach when a great storm came up, and rain poured down violently. It rained so hard that Sir Griflet had to stop and find shelter under an oak tree at the top of a hill. From there, he saw a boat approach the shore. He saw some ladies come ashore (he thought he recognized Morgana le Fay among them). They picked up King Arthur's body and took it to the ship, which set sail immediately and disappeared on the horizon. Some say it sailed to the island of Avalon, where King Arthur is buried.

THE RETURN OF LAUNCELOT

When he found out what had happened in the realm of Logris, Sir Launcelot remained speechless. For an entire day he wandered alone through the forests of Ganis. Then he returned to his palace and ordered that a regiment be prepared, and ships as well, that would set sail immediately for the shores of Great Britain.

It was a very sorrowful trip, and Sir Launcelot continued to ask himself, "Could King Arthur really have died? And has the flame of the knighthood been spent forever? And what could have happened to beautiful Guinevere, my gentle and beloved queen?"

Finally the boats reached Great Britain, arriving right at the plain of Salisbury, where the final battle had taken place. Sir Launcelot, Sir Ector, Sir Lionel and others came ashore and went slowly ahead. What a horrible sight! Sir Launcelot wandered about for some time, crying and asking himself, "Could these really have been the weapons of Sir Sagramour, and this

bald skull the head of Sir Segurade? Oh what a terrible fate! If everyone has died, then this really is the end of the enchantment and the wonderful adventures forever and ever."

The next day, as he went to pray in the chapel not far from the sea, he met a pious monk who said to him, "Sir Launcelot, you should know that right in this very place King Arthur gave his soul to God. Of his many knights, only Sir Griflet le fise de Dieu was saved. Unfortunately he died ten days later of his many wounds."

"And the queen? What has happened to the queen?" asked Sir Launcelot.

"She locked herself in the Joyous Gard. After hearing of the battle, Queen Guinevere left and became a nun in the convent of Saint Clarence."

Sir Launcelot left with great sadness in his heart, and letting his horse choose the way, he wandered for an entire day. Night was falling when Sir Ector, who was with him, said, "Where do you want to go, my friend? You have wandered for too long." "You are right," said Sir Launcelot. "The time has come. Go back with all of the men to the realm of Ganis, and there I shall make you king." This surprised and disoriented Sir Ector, who said, "And what will become of you?"

"Whatever God shall wish," said Sir Launcelot. He tearfully hugged his companion goodbye, and then turned and went along his way.

THE END OF LAUNCELOT

A few days later, Sir Launcelot arrived at an ancient monastery, from which twenty monks in white came out to welcome him. These monks were actually all of the great knights who realized, after the battle of Salisbury, that the era had come to an end. And so they retired to this abbey, to prepare to finally one day meet God, the greatest of all kings. "And so I shall do the same," thought Sir Launcelot.

After one year, he received the news that Queen Guinevere had died. He was deeply absorbed in prayer and meditation. Some time later, his soul finally went to join God. Sir Launcelot was brought to the castle of the Joyous Gard, and was buried there. The people of the castle, together with the peasants from the nearby lands brought flowers to his tomb without fail each and every single day.